The Sea Unicorn

The Sea Keepers series

The Sea Unicorn

CORAL RIPLEY

sourcebooks
young readers

Published by Sourcebooks Young Readers, an imprint of Sourcebooks Kids
P.O. Box 4410, Naperville, Illinois 60567-4410
(630) 961-3900
sourcebookskids.com

Originally published as *The Sea Keepers: The Sea Unicorn* in 2020 in Great
Britain by Orchard Books, an imprint of Hachette Children's Group.

Library of Congress Cataloging-in-Publication Data is on file with the
publisher.

Source of Production: Sheridan Books, Chelsea, Michigan, United States
Date of Production: March 2021
Run Number: 5021072

Printed and bound in the United States of America.
SB 10 9 8 7 6 5 4 3 2 1

Special thanks to Sarah Hawkins.

For Lyla Rivers, who has the
best mermaid name ever.

Chapter One

"Hey, wait for me!" Layla flicked her turquoise tail and swam after her mermaid friends. She laughed as she caught up with them and they spun around in a circle...

"Layla! Stop daydreaming!" Grace laughed.

Layla shook her head and looked around. She wasn't underwater; she was in her kitchen, sitting at the table with her best friends with their homework spread out in front of them.

"Were you thinking about the mermaids?" Emily asked.

"Shhh!" Grace said, looking over at where Layla's dad and her big sister, Nadia, were making dinner.

Luckily, Dad was busy reading a recipe, and Nadia had her earphones in. "*Oooh yeah, I loooooooveeee you,*" she sang, dancing around as she chopped an onion.

The girls giggled. Layla beckoned to her friends, and they put their heads so close that Layla's straight, dark hair was almost touching Emily's black curls and Grace's long blond hair. "I was thinking about the mermaids," she whispered. "I wish our bracelets would glow so we could visit them again!"

Layla didn't just daydream about

mermaids; she really did have adventures with them!

It had all started when she, Emily, and Grace had rescued a dolphin called Kai, who had turned out to be the pet of Marina, a mermaid princess. Marina was the coolest person Layla had ever met. She had taken the girls to her palace in the incredible underwater kingdom of Atlantis. There, to everyone's surprise, Layla, Grace, and Emily had been chosen to become Sea Keepers—the only ones who could find the Golden Pearls and save Atlantis from the evil siren, Effluvia. Ever since they had returned home, the three friends had been waiting for the magic shell bracelets Marina had given them to glow and take them on another mermaid adventure!

"You're daydreaming again!" Grace said.

Layla stuck her tongue out at her friend.

"Come on," Emily told them, "we've got to figure out what we're going to do for our project!"

Layla gave a dramatic sigh, but she

picked up the homework sheet and tried to read what it said. There were some really long words.

"Okay, so maybe we could do a poster, or a presentation—" Grace started.

"Wait a second," Layla told her, frowning as she concentrated on the words.

"Oh, sorry," Grace said. "I forgot."

"What's wrong?" Emily asked.

Sometimes Layla had to remind herself she hadn't known Emily that long. Emily had only moved to their seaside town recently.

"It takes me a little longer because I have dyslexia," Layla explained. "The letters get all muddled. But I'm good at other things—like solving problems."

"Do you want me to read it for you?" Emily offered. Layla shook her head.

"I can do it," she said. She ran her fingers under each word, like she'd been taught, breaking the tricky words into smaller parts.

"*Around the world, children have been going on strike from school to protest about global warming,*" she read. "*Make a project to tell people about environmental challenges. Be imaginative.*"

"What's global warming again?" Grace asked.

"It means the world's getting hotter because people are polluting it by producing too many greenhouse gases, like carbon dioxide. The gases stay in the atmosphere and make the whole world warmer," Emily explained.

"*Ooooooohhh—eeeeehhhh—oooohhh!*"

Nadia sang from the kitchen. The girls laughed.

"Maybe we can write a global warming song?" Layla suggested. She loved to sing and dance. "We could perform it at school!"

"No way!" Emily shook her head.

"I don't have a very good voice," Grace said.

"That's not stopping my sister," Layla joked. "We need to do something fun, though. Ooh! How about a video?" she suggested. "We can film it with my dad's phone. I can be the star!" She held her arms above her head and did a wriggle that made her friends laugh.

"Sounds more fun than a poster," Grace said.

"And less writing," Layla said, grinning.

"I'll be the one who films it!" Emily agreed.

"Hey, Dad—can I borrow your phone?" Layla asked.

Her father shook his head. "Sorry Lay, I'm on call tonight." Layla's parents were both doctors. "Ask your mom."

"Mooooom! Can I borrow your phone?" Layla called, leading Emily and Grace into the family room. Mom's hands were on the floor, with her bottom stuck up in the air. "Oops, sorry," Layla giggled. "Can I borrow your phone? It's for our homework."

"Layla, I'm doing yoga here," Mom grumbled, but she pointed to where her phone was lying on the sofa.

"Thanks!" Layla grabbed it, and the girls ran upstairs to her room. "Sorry about the

mess," she said. Emily and Grace grinned at each other. Layla's room was always a mess. Today there was a slime-making kit scattered all over the floor, unicorn stuffed animals piled on the bed, and a feather boa spilling out of her wardrobe.

"Maybe we can dress up for the video!" Layla said, flinging things out of her dress-up box. "I could be a news anchor.

 9

From the future!" she added as she put on a sparkly sequin hat.

"Layla," Emily said.

"Okay, you can be the news anchor," Layla said, still rummaging through the box.

"Layla!" Grace said urgently.

Layla turned to see her friends hopping around excitedly. She gave a squeal when she realized why. Their bracelets were glowing—they were going on another mermaid adventure!

The girls held hands and looked down at their shell bracelets. They remembered exactly what to do because they'd talked about it every day since their last adventure. Nobody would worry about them while they were gone, because no time would pass here while they were in the mermaid kingdom.

Together, they chanted the magic words:

"Take me to the ocean blue,
Sea Keepers to the rescue!"

Instantly, blue bubbles appeared in the air around them, swirling like a magical whirlwind. The air sparkled with magic,

 11

and Layla felt a tugging on her clothes. Then—POP!—they were underwater!

Layla looked down at her beautiful turquoise tail. It was covered in tiny scales in all shades of blue and green, and her fins were coral-pink with sparkly turquoise tips. She swished her tail happily and admired how it shimmered in the water. Then Grace and Emily grabbed her hands and the girls swam around in a circle, whooping in delight, just like Layla had imagined. They were mermaids!

"Brrr!" said Layla.

Emily nodded, her teeth chattering. "The water's sooooo chilly!"

"Welcome back, Sea Keepers!" a familiar voice called from behind them.

The girls turned to see a mermaid

with pink-and-purple hair and a tail with different shades of purple swimming nearby.

"Marina!" they all cried. The girls crowded around to hug their friend.

"How are you? We're not in Atlantis, are we? It's freezing here! Where are we?" Questions spilled out of Layla.

"Come and find out!" Marina said, her eyes twinkling. She flicked her tail and shot toward the surface. Grinning excitedly, the girls followed her.

As their heads went above water, Layla shivered. It was freezing—literally! Floating ice sparkled brightly in the sunshine, and there was glistening white snow everywhere.

"Welcome to the Arctic!" Marina said.

Chapter Two

"This is amazing!" Layla said, looking around at the beautiful frozen scene in front of them.

"Look!" Emily squealed.

Layla turned to see some seals resting on a nearby iceberg. The seals stared back at them with big, brown eyes. Then one started to wriggle toward the edge of the ice, flopping forward on her tummy. With a plop she dove into the water, followed by another, and another.

The girls dove underwater to see them.

On the ice, the seals had been slow and awkward, but in the water they were sleek and quick, their long whiskers twitching as they spun and flipped, changing directions with just a flick of their tails.

"Hi!" Layla called as one swam past.

"Welcome, Sea Keepers," the seal said.

Layla put out her hand and stroked her head, and the seal snuffled into her arm. Layla giggled—her whiskers tickled!

Beside her, Emily stroked another seal, while sporty Grace raced a group of them around the sparkling iceberg.

"Mmm, you're nice and warm!" Layla exclaimed as the seal snuggled against her.

"Are you cold?" Marina asked.

 17

"Freezing my tail off!" Layla said.

"That's why Kai stayed in Atlantis," Marina told her. "Dolphins hate the cold. Here, let me warm you up a little." She spread her hands around in the water, and it swirled with color. The girls grinned at each other. Marina was going to do magic!

Their mermaid friend sang:

**"In this place of ice and storm,
Keep these girls toasty warm!"**

The water around Emily, Grace, and Layla shimmered with all the colors of the rainbow, and suddenly Layla felt cozy and warm. Marina's magic was protecting them from the cold!

"Mmm, that's better," Grace said.

"I'm glad you're here," Layla said.

"Why are we here?" Emily asked. "Has the Mystic Clam remembered where another Golden Pearl is hidden?"

Marina nodded. "He told me a riddle." She flicked her tail as she recited:

"To find the pearl you must be bold,
And swim in waters icy cold,
Where water's frozen in the air,
A Golden Pearl is waiting there!"

"Water frozen in the air..." Layla repeated thoughtfully. But before she could figure the riddle out, there was a commotion from the seals. A new creature had arrived, but it wasn't like any animal

  19

Layla had ever seen before. He looked like a small, speckled gray whale, but he had a horn like a unicorn!

"What is that?" Layla breathed.

"Oh, it's a narwhal!" Emily squealed. She loved animals and knew lots of facts about them.

"That's only a young one," Marina explained. "They get much bigger, and

their tusks grow even longer than their bodies. They usually live in groups called pods. I wonder where the rest of his family is?"

"Wow!" Grace breathed, admiring the narwhal's beautiful tusk. "A sea unicorn!"

"First we met mermaids, now unicorns!" Layla grinned. "We're the luckiest girls in the world!"

But there was something wrong. The narwhal swam over to them awkwardly, only moving one of his flippers.

"Ow, ow, ow, owwww!" he cried.

"Oh no, are you okay?" Emily asked as they all swam over.

"My flipper," the narwhal said, holding it up awkwardly. "I think it's broken. Please, help me!"

"Of course we will," Layla said. "What's your name? I'm Layla, and this is Grace, Emily, and Marina."

"Oh, thank you!" the narwhal said. "I'm Harper."

As Marina gently touched the narwhal's flipper while she was examining it, Harper let out a heart-wrenching howl of pain.

Emily stroked the narwhal's side sympathetically. "You poor thing, that must really hurt!"

"Hmm, I think you need medical attention," Marina said. "Let's go to the Ice Palace Animal Sanctuary. The Arctic mermaids can help you!"

"The Ice Palace Animal Sanctuary?" Layla echoed.

"Arctic mermaids?" Grace added. The

girls all grinned at one another. It sounded incredible!

But Harper looked nervous. "Oh, don't worry, I'm sure you were doing something important. I wouldn't want to keep you. Where are you going?"

"It's okay, we want to help," Grace reassured her.

"In fact, we have to help—that's what Sea Keepers do!" Layla joked.

"Thank you," the little narwhal said. Layla put an arm around him to help him swim along.

"This way," Marina said.

Up ahead, the ice completely covered the surface, making the water below dark green, almost black. Unlike the waters near Atlantis, which were full of mermaids and

all kinds of underwater creatures, there was barely anyone around. The waters were eerily quiet and still, and the girls found themselves whispering as they went along.

"Has Effluvia caused any trouble lately?" Grace whispered to Marina.

Marina shook her head, her hair swirling in the water. "There's been no sign of her since you found the pearl the last time you were here," she told them.

Layla shuddered as she thought about Effluvia, the evil siren who wanted to take over Atlantis. Sirens were a type of mermaid whose songs could enchant anyone into doing what they wanted. The sirens had tried to steal the Golden Pearls and use their magic to take over Atlantis once before.

There had been a great battle, and after the mermaids won, Queen Nerissa, Marina's ancestor, had banished all the sirens to the deepest part of the ocean.

After they were gone, Queen Nerissa had hidden the Golden Pearls across the seven seas so that no one could use them for evil again. But Effluvia had escaped,

 25

and now she was determined to find a Golden Pearl and use its magic to release her sisters and take over Atlantis—forever!

The Sea Keepers' job was to find the Golden Pearls before Effluvia did and use their power to help the mermaids and sea creatures. Unfortunately, only the Mystic Clam was old enough to remember where the pearls were hidden!

Layla glanced behind her as she and Harper swam along. Thinking about Effluvia was making her nervous! It didn't help that the Arctic water was so dark. With luminous starfish dotted around, glowing in the dark, it was almost like they were swimming through the night sky.

As they swam on, Layla noticed a shaft of light coming from the surface.

"That's a breathing hole," Harper explained. "Narwhals, seals, and whales have to go to the surface to breathe—but polar bears know that and wait there to attack!"

 27

Layla gasped in fright. She felt very lucky that mermaids could breathe underwater!

"The Arctic is a dangerous place," Marina told them. "That's why the sanctuary is so important." She pointed in the distance. "There it is!"

The girls looked up—and up and up! The sanctuary was an enormous palace that towered up from the seabed and reached high above the frozen surface.

It looked like a fairy-tale palace, with spiraling turrets and beautiful balconies, but it was completely made out of glittering ice!

"It used to be the winter palace of my great-great grandfather, King Triton," Marina explained, "but he gave it to the

Arctic mermaids so that they could help creatures in need."

"It's wonderful!" Grace breathed.

But as they approached the doors, there was a shout that echoed across the empty water.

"HALT! Who goes there!" A mermaid and a merman swam out. The merman had a white tail and long white hair, and the mermaid had a silver tail and pale blue hair. They had fierce expressions on their faces—and they were both holding massive spears!

Chapter Three

The girls froze as the Arctic merpeople swam toward them, pointing their spears threateningly. Harper ducked behind the girls, even though his tusk stuck out and gave her hiding place away.

"Hello!" Layla said, trying to sound friendly. "We're the Sea Keepers, and this is Princess Marina."

"We've brought an injured narwhal to the sanctuary," Emily added.

"And we're looking for a Golden Pearl," Grace chimed in.

The mermaid lowered her spear and swam forward, a look of concern on her face. She gently examined Harper's flipper. As she did, Layla noticed that she was wearing a delicate tiara made of sparkling ice crystals.

"Hmm, I don't think it's broken. Let's go inside and we can check it properly," she said.

Layla gave a sigh of relief. The Arctic

mermaids looked fierce, but they were just as kind as every other mermaid they'd met so far.

"I'm Toklo, and this is Anji, our leader," the merman said, lowering his spear.

Layla looked at Anji in surprise. She didn't look much older than them, and under the tiara her long blue hair was in braids.

"But you're so young!" she blurted out.

Anji laughed and nodded. "I'm the youngest leader the Arctic merfolk have ever had."

"And the bravest," Toklo added with a grin.

Layla couldn't stop sneaking peeks at Anji's spear as the Sea Keepers helped Harper swim though the palace doors. It was longer than she was tall, and it was

covered in a beautiful swirling pattern.

"Is that a narwhal tusk?" she asked. Harper nodded.

"When a narwhal dies, he leaves his tusk to the Arctic merpeople. It is a great honor to carry one," Toklo told them, bowing to Harper.

"Useful too," Anji added. "These waters are dangerous—that's why we always need to be on guard. A polar bear or orca might eat a mermaid if they have no other choice."

The girls looked at one another

nervously. Suddenly the Arctic felt a lot less safe than Atlantis!

"Don't worry, you'll be safe in here," Anji laughed. She led them inside the palace. The girls stared in amazement as they went into a vast hall with huge pillars holding up a high, vaulted ice ceiling. It was lit by glowing green algae and luminous starfish. And all around, there were mermaids! Unlike the Atlantis mermaids, whose tails were brightly colored, the Arctic mermaids had shimmering silver, white, and pale blue tails, and they all wore glittering jewelry made of ice crystals.

"It's so hot!" complained a mermaid, fanning herself with her blue tail.

"I know," said a merman holding a gorgeous narwhal tusk. "I'm boiling."

"How can they be hot?" Layla exclaimed.

"It might feel chilly to you," Anji said, "but it is meant to be even colder. My great-grandparents had icicles in their eyebrows all day long and their hair was always frozen solid!" She shook her head sadly. "It's getting warmer and warmer every year. The Arctic ice is gradually melting, and we just don't know why. Even the palace is slowly melting. One day, it will be gone forever!"

Layla felt a knot in her tummy. "Oh no," she whispered to her friends. "It's because of global warming!"

Before the others could reply, Anji took them through the great hall and out into a huge courtyard of open water. But it was completely different than the quiet water outside the sanctuary. There were creatures everywhere, laughing and playing!

Anji saw their amazed faces and smiled. "Come look at this," she said, taking them to the surface. Their heads popped above water in a beautiful clear pool surrounded by snow and ice. And on the snow, there were creatures of all kinds—rabbits, snow owls, walruses, and foxes, all playing together.

Mermaids perched on the ice were busy changing bandages, feeding baby animals, and giving cuddles.

"Aww!" Layla squealed. She had just spotted some seal pups so white and fluffy that they almost blended in with the snow.

"Look, polar bear cubs too!" Grace

cried out, pointing to where a mother polar bear was rolling around with her three adorable cubs.

"They won't hurt the seals, will they?" worried Emily.

"Outside, they would," Toklo told her, "but in the sanctuary they've sworn not to hurt another creature. They are all under our magical protection."

"These creatures are here because they have been injured, are starving, or have babies and need a safe space—and our help—until they get better," Anji said. "Like you," she added, smiling at Harper. "We should get someone to look at your flipper."

But Harper swam behind Layla nervously.

"Can I stay with the Sea Keepers?" he asked.

"Don't worry, we'll come with you," Layla reassured her.

"I just need to check on some other patients first," Anji said, pulling herself up onto the nearest ice floe and stroking an Arctic rabbit with a splint on his leg.

One of the polar bear cubs raced over the ice to get into Anji's lap, and a fluffy white baby seal flopped over to her, making happy snuffling noises.

"Awwww!" Emily said. She pulled herself up on the ice too and started playing with the polar bear cub. Then Grace swung herself up onto the ice and petted the rabbit.

"Well, I'm not going to miss out on

cuddling baby animals!" Layla said, pulling herself out next to the others. Marina stayed in the water with Harper, leaning her elbows on the ice.

Layla shuffled onto the ice, feeling like one of the seals flopping around. It was a lot harder to move on land when you didn't have legs! She perched on the ice, her tail still in the water, and stroked the seal cub's fur. "Their fur is so fluffy and soft!" she said, grinning.

"This is their baby fur," Anji explained. "It's not waterproof yet, so they can't swim until they get their adult coats."

Emily stroked a polar bear cub, and she rolled over onto her back.

"My dog Barkley does that when he wants his tummy tickled," Grace told her.

Emily tickled the cub's soft tummy and she wriggled in delight. The girls all laughed.

"You'll be back home at the Frozen Falls in no time," Anji told the mother polar bear.

That's it! Layla splashed the water with her tail, sending shimmering droplets up into the icy air.

"Are you okay?" Grace asked.

"Yes!" said Layla. "I think I know where the pearl is." She turned to Anji. "Are you talking about a frozen waterfall?"

Anji nodded.

"That must be the place in the riddle!" Layla exclaimed. "*Where water's frozen in the air, a Golden Pearl is waiting there!*"

"Good thinking, Layla!" Emily exclaimed.

Down in the water, Harper jerked his head around so quickly that Layla had to duck to avoid getting poked by the narwhal's tusk.

"Oh dear," Grace asked, peering down at him. "Is your flipper hurting?"

"Um, yes," Harper said. "Ow!"

"The falls are just beyond a breathing hole on the other side of the ice mountains," said Anji. "Let's get Harper's flipper checked out, and then I'll take you all there."

"Actually, I'm feeling much better—"

 4 3

Harper started. But he was interrupted by a huge thud. Vibrations rippled through the water. A deadly hush fell over the sanctuary.

Moments later, shouts of "Help!" rang out from the great hall.

"What's going on?" asked Layla.

"The sanctuary is under attack!" Anji cried out.

Chapter Four

At once, the Arctic mermaids grabbed their spears and dove down through the water. Marina and the girls followed, Harper trailing behind them.

"Who would attack the sanctuary?" Anji asked as they swam.

Layla, Grace, and Emily groaned—they had an idea who it might be...

They all swam back to the great hall.

A crowd of merpeople were gathered around the palace doors, watching in horror as the ice shook with each enormous thud. There was another thud, which echoed though the hall, and a crack appeared in the door. Through the crack, they could see a giant orca smashing his head into the ice!

The mermaids looked shocked.

"Why would an orca attack the sanctuary? We help them here too!" Anji said, looking upset.

"He must be under Effluvia's spell," Grace explained.

"Her singing can make you do whatever she wants," Emily told them with a shudder. The girls knew how it felt— Effluvia had almost put them under her spell before, but luckily Marina and some dolphins had managed to stop her.

"Everyone! Gather your spears!" Anji ordered. "Fetch any able sea creature. We must defend the sanctuary!"

Before they could move, there was an enormous crash. The ice doors shattered into a million sparkling pieces, and Effluvia and her enormous orca swam into the great hall.

"Sea Keepers!" she called. "Oh, Sea Keepers, where are you?" Effluvia smiled slyly when she saw the girls. "Ah, there you are."

Her voice was so high and lilting that
she sounded like an angel or a fairy. It
was hard to believe that she was evil, but
that was all part of a siren's power. Her
long blue hair spread out around her, and
her dark purple tail flicked from side to
side. Effluvia's nasty pet anglerfish, Fang,

swam next to her, a glowing light dangling from her head. She grinned menacingly, showing her sharp teeth.

Emily nudged Layla and Grace. "Look at her eyes," she whispered, pointing at the orca. The great black-and-white whale had the same light in his eyes as the giant squid that Effluvia had enchanted before. The orca was under the siren's spell, and that made him very dangerous—he would do anything Effluvia asked.

Anji swam forward, her spear pointed at Effluvia. "You are not welcome here. Leave now while you have the chance."

Effluvia ignored her. "You have something that belongs to me."

Layla, Emily, and Grace glanced at each other uncertainly. Did she mean the pearl?

4 9

Effluvia threw her head back and laughed. "Come, my little spy," she called, looking over at Harper, who moved closer to Layla.

"It's okay," Layla murmured, reaching down to comfort the narwhal. "We won't let her hurt you."

"I'm sorry," Harper whispered. Then he swam over to Effluvia, moving gracefully through the water.

Everyone gasped.

Layla stared at the narwhal in shock. Harper's flipper wasn't hurt at all—he was a spy!

"I can't believe he lied to us about his injured flipper," Emily said, looking as if she was about to cry.

"That's not the worst thing," Grace

said grimly. "Harper was there when I told Anji the riddle!"

"Have you found out where the pearl is?" Effluvia snapped.

Harper gave a small nod.

"Tell me!" Effluvia demanded.

Harper stared at the girls hesitantly. "But, Effluvia—"

"Tell me!" Effluvia shouted. "Or do you want to end up as my orca's snack?"

The orca grinned nastily, showing his sharp teeth.

Harper shivered. "The pearl is hidden at the Frozen Falls," he whispered.

"I know where that is," the orca growled.

"Even if you know where the pearl is, it doesn't mean that you'll find it before we do," Grace said defiantly. "The Arctic mermaids will help us look!"

"Oh, I think they'll be busy...trying to save their precious sanctuary." Effluvia pointed at the palace and let out a high note that reverberated around the icy walls. Magic shimmered through the water as she sang:

"My heart's colder than it's ever felt,
Make this sanctuary quickly melt!"

The Sea Keepers and Marina looked at one another in horror.

The sanctuary was going to be destroyed!

Chapter Five

Everyone watched in dismay as the walls of the palace began to melt. Effluvia laughed as she swam away, Harper trailing after her. As the orca left, he sniggered and thumped the wall of the great hall with his huge tail. A crack appeared in the weakened ice.

"Mermaids, use your magic!" Anji commanded. "Fix what you can!"

"We have to help them!" Emily cried.

Marina shook her head. "Things will

get a lot worse if Effluvia gets the pearl and the sirens rule the seas," she said.

"And if we get the Golden Pearl, we can use its magic to save the sanctuary," Grace added.

"We *have* to get to the Frozen Falls before Effluvia," Layla said.

"I'm sorry, I can't spare anyone to guide you," Anji said. "I need every mermaid and merman to try and save the sanctuary..."

They watched the crack as it spread up the wall and into the ceiling like a lightning bolt. Three mermaids swam over, using their magic to patch it up. As they worked to repair the damage, more cracks appeared!

"But Effluvia hasn't thought of everything," Anji continued. "I can help you without leaving the sanctuary!" She closed her eyes and held her narwhal spear up proudly. Then she began to sing, her voice echoing around the melting palace:

"Arctic starfish, hear my calls,
Lead them to the Frozen Falls!"

 5 7

"Follow the starfish, Sea Keepers!" Anji called as she swam over to help the others. "Good luck!"

"Let's go!" Grace shouted, heading toward the broken doors. As they swam through the great hall, there was a horrible creaking sound and another crack appeared above the entrance. A mermaid swam up to start fixing it.

Suddenly there was a huge noise, like thunder.

"Look out!" Grace yelled.

As a chunk of ice fell, she pushed Layla and Emily out of the way just in time. The ice crashed down where they had been swimming a second before.

"Thanks, Grace," Layla said, feeling a little shaky.

Emily nodded; her eyes wide. "That was close."

"We've got to get out of here!" Marina cried as more and more ice broke away from the ceiling.

"Everyone into the courtyard!" Anji commanded.

The Arctic mermaids followed their leader's order, and Marina and the girls swam in the opposite direction, toward the palace doors, dodging massive chunks of ice as they came crashing down all around them. When they had almost reached the exit, Layla heard a cry.

One mermaid hadn't managed to avoid the falling ceiling, and her fins were trapped under a huge chunk of ice. She was trying desperately to lift it up, but the ice was too heavy.

"We've got to help her!" cried Layla.

Marina and the Sea Keepers swam over.

The trapped mermaid shook her head.

"You have to go; the whole ceiling is going to cave in!"

"We can't leave you here," Emily said.

"Everyone, lift!" ordered Grace. They heaved the ice block high enough for the mermaid to pull out her fins.

"Come on!" shouted Layla. "Let's go!"

They all swam out of the doorway— and just in time too. As they escaped, there was a huge creak and the rest of the ceiling tumbled down, smashing onto the seabed with such force that it sent a shock wave through the water.

"Thank you," the mermaid said, looking as pale as her ice-white hair.

As she went to join the other mermaids in the courtyard, the girls and Marina surfaced and watched one of the turrets topple into the icy waters.

"The poor sanctuary," Emily said. She looked close to tears.

"We'll fix it," Grace said. "But first we need to find that pearl!"

"Follow the starfish..." Layla muttered as they dove underwater.

"There!" Grace pointed to a starfish down on the rocky seabed. It wiggled one of its legs, pointing the girls to the left.

"There's another one!" Layla cried out as she spotted a starfish glow up ahead.

The luminous orange starfish pointed the way to the Frozen Falls.

"Thank you, thank you!" Emily called to each starfish they passed as they swam through the icy waters.

"Yes!" Grace cheered as she pointed to another starfish. "I've spotted eight, Emily and Marina have each spotted five and Layla's only spotted one!"

"It's not a contest, Grace," Marina said, laughing.

"If it was, Layla would be losing," Grace joked, nudging her with her tail.

Layla tried to laugh. The truth was

she couldn't concentrate on spotting the starfish, because she had the oddest sensation that there was someone following her. She turned and looked, but there was no one there. She told herself not to be silly. *It's just because it's dark and spooky down here*, she thought. But when she glanced behind her again, Grace and Emily noticed.

"What's wrong?" Grace asked her.

"I just feel like we're being followed," Layla said, shivering.

All three girls turned and looked behind them. The water was as silent as it had been before, and the only thing they could see were the icebergs jutting down from the ice overhead like the frozen teeth of a sea monster.

"Actually, I know what you mean,"

Grace murmured. "I've got the heebie-jeebies too."

Emily clutched Layla's hand, and Layla squeezed it reassuringly.

"Maybe it's another one of Effluvia's spies," Marina said crossly. "I still can't believe Harper was working for her!"

"He wasn't hypnotized like the orca, because his eyes weren't glowing," Grace said as they swam.

"He seemed so nice," Emily said. "Maybe Effluvia did something else to force him..."

Layla gave Emily's hand another squeeze. Emily was so kind! She always thought the best of everyone. But maybe Harper was just bad, like Effluvia? Layla shook her head. Right now, they had to

concentrate on getting the Golden Pearl.
She scanned the rocky seabed up ahead.

"There!" she said, spotting another
starfish, lit up in the light from a breathing
hole up ahead.

"Didn't Anji say the Frozen Falls were
near a breathing hole?" Emily said. "We're
almost there!"

But as they swam toward it, something made Layla turn around. Out of the corner of her eye she saw a flash of something gray before it disappeared behind an iceberg. There *was* someone following them!

Chapter Six

"Aha!" Layla cried as she recognized the speckled creature trying to hide behind the iceberg. "I can see your tusk, Harper!"

The little narwhal swam cautiously out from his hiding place.

"Why are you following us? What do you want now?" Marina said crossly as she, Grace, and Emily swam over.

"I'm so sorry I told Effluvia where the pearl is hidden." Harper hung his head in shame. "I lost my family, and I was all alone.

When Effluvia found me, she said I had to do what she told me or she'd let the orca eat me. I was scared." The narwhal began to cry.

As the girls crowded around Harper to reassure him, Layla felt a burst of relief that the sea unicorn wasn't bad after all. "You should have told us. We'd never let anything happen to you," she said.

"I'd be scared without my family too," Marina said. "Even though my brother, Prince Neptune, is a real pain!"

The girls laughed, and even Harper stopped crying. "I just want to help you," he said, looking at them, his eyes wide.

"Well, come on then! Last one to spot a starfish is a rotten egg!" Grace said.

As they neared a breathing hole, a baby seal swam up to them like an excited puppy.

The seal's mother raced up behind her. "Freya!" she scolded. "What did I say about swimming off?"

"Sorry, Mama," Freya said. "This is my first swim!" she told the Sea Keepers. "I just lost my baby fur!"

"You're a great swimmer!" Layla told her.

"And your new fur is lovely," added Emily. The little seal proudly puffed out her chest.

Freya's mom pointed up at the breathing hole. "We'll go up and take a breath, then come straight back down. No messing around."

Freya nodded obediently, her whiskers quivering with excitement.

As the two seals swam toward the surface, Layla noticed a shadow overhead. "What's that?"

Next to her, Harper gasped. "It's probably a polar bear," he said shakily.

"Are you sure?" Emily asked.

The sea unicorn nodded. "I think so."

"Sea Keepers!" Marina pulled the girls to one side. "It could be another trick," she

 7 2

whispered anxiously. "Effluvia could have sent Harper to distract us so she can find the pearl before we get there."

The Sea Keepers exchanged worried looks. Layla didn't know what to do.

They had to find the Golden Pearl—the Arctic mermaids desperately needed their help. Every second was precious, but they couldn't leave the seals in danger.

She glanced over at Harper. Somehow, she trusted him. The little narwhal had made a mistake, but he seemed genuinely sorry. Now he was trying to make up for it—or at least Layla really hoped so!

"I believe Harper," Layla said.

Emily and Grace nodded.

"We've got to warn the seals," said Grace, taking off after them.

There was no time to lose—the two seals had almost reached the surface! Layla flicked her fins as fast as she could, wishing she could swim as quickly as Grace. Then Layla remembered something—she wasn't as speedy as her friend, but she was much louder!

"Freya!" she yelled. "STOP!"

The mother and baby halted, just beneath the surface, and turned to wait for them to catch up.

As they joined the seals, Layla peered up at the breathing hole, looking for a sign of movement from the ice above. Everything was perfectly still. Had the polar bear gone away? Or had Harper made the whole thing up?

"We thought there was a polar— *argh!*" Layla shrieked as a huge white paw swiped down into the water, sharp claws outstretched toward Freya!

Lowering his head, Harper swam forward and charged at the polar bear's

paw with his tusk. The bear let out a yelp and yanked its paw out of the water. Marina and the Sea Keepers quickly pulled Freya and her mom to safety.

"Phew!" said Freya, her eyes wide. "My first swim was nearly my last!"

"Is everyone okay?" asked Harper, swimming over to them.

Layla nodded shakily. It had been a *very* close call.

"Thank you so much," the mother seal said. "You saved our lives."

"I'm sorry I didn't trust you," Marina apologized to Harper. "What you did was very brave."

"It's okay," Harper said. "I'm just glad Freya's all right."

"She might not be much longer if Effluvia gets that pearl!" Grace said with concern. "Now come on—we need to get to the Frozen Falls!"

Waving goodbye to the seals, they swam on as fast as they could, trying to make up for lost time. Layla's tummy flipped nervously as she thought about the Golden Pearl. What if Effluvia had already found it?

"Starfish!" Grace called from up

ahead. But this starfish wasn't pointing left or right. Instead it pointed up, toward the surface. Sure enough, they could see light streaming down from a break in the ice.

"I just hope we're not too late!" Layla said.

Just then, she heard a familiar voice carrying through the water. "I thought you knew where it was, blubber brain! We've been going around in circles!" The girls grinned. There was only one person who would be so rude—Effluvia!

They peered around the iceberg and saw Effluvia with Fang and the enormous orca.

"It's above the surface," the orca said grumpily.

"Finally, a Golden Pearl will be mine!" Effluvia crowed.

"Not if we get to it first!" Grace called.

"Two-legs!" Effluvia spun around to look at them. "And the useless pinhead too. So you found each other, how nice! Well, there's nothing you can do. Soon the pearl will be mine, and my siren sisters will rule the oceans!" Effluvia laughed as she shot up to the surface.

"After her!" Layla yelled. They'd come so far; they couldn't let Effluvia get the pearl now!

The Sea Keepers poked their heads out of the water and looked around the icy landscape. They were in a vast circle of water, surrounded by great mountains of ice. In front of them was a frozen waterfall, cascading icicles that spiked into the water like a huge wall of blue glass. And from high above the water came a golden glow!

Chapter Seven

"The Golden Pearl," Effluvia breathed as they stared up at the frozen waterfall. The pearl was embedded deep in the ice.

"But it's out of the water!" Marina cried. "No one can get it up there!"

"I know who can—some *two-legs!*" Layla realized in delight. "Marina, if you turn us back into humans, we can climb up and get the pearl! Thanks for the idea, Effluvia," she added, cheekily.

"No!" Effluvia howled. "Don't let them

near those falls!" She pointed her finger at the orca and sang a high, piercing note. The hypnotized light in the orca's eyes grew even brighter. He swam over to where the Frozen Falls jutted into the water and swam in front of the ice menacingly.

"I bet I can get past the orca!" Grace took off impulsively. She sped through the water, darting to one side so that the orca moved to block her, then changing direction at the last minute.

Grace was fast, but the orca was faster. He swept her away with his tail, sending her spinning off through the water.

"Grace!" Layla, Marina, and Emily rushed over to their friend.

Grace swam over and shook her head. "It's no good," she said.

Effluvia laughed wickedly.

"What are we going to do?" Marina asked the Sea Keepers.

But someone else was speeding toward the black-and-white whale—the little narwhal!

"Harper, no!" Layla called.

But the narwhal was determined. "I'll

deal with the orca!" he called. "You get that pearl!"

Layla held her breath as she watched the narwhal swim bravely toward the much-bigger orca.

"What are you doing, you floating toothpick?" Effluvia yelled. "My orca's going to eat you in one mouthful!"

"I'm doing what I should have done all along!" Harper said. "Helping the Sea Keepers!"

The orca had his eyes fixed on Harper hungrily. As the narwhal swam up, the orca lashed out and chomped at him. The girls gasped, but Harper was quick and dodged out of the way just in time. The orca tried to smash him with a whack from his great tail, but Harper darted out of reach.

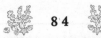

He dipped and dove around the orca, poking him with the pointy tip of his tusk. Giving a loud bellow, the orca lunged after him. Harper swam off, and the enormous orca chased her, swimming away from the Frozen Falls.

Now was their chance!

"Go, Sea Keepers!" Harper cried. "I'll hold off the orca!"

"No!" Effluvia shrieked. She sped toward the edge of the water, but the girls were there first. They pulled themselves up onto the spiky ice.

Marina quickly sang out:

"Magic of snow and icy freeze,
Make these girls human, please!"

The water around the girls' tails shimmered as they turned back into legs. Marina's magic had also given them thick snowsuits and boots, to keep them warm above the water's surface. The girls scrambled onto the ice, slipping and sliding as they went. Layla held her arms out, trying to keep her balance as she walked. If she fell, she'd topple into the freezing-cold water!

"There it is!" Grace called, pointing up at the glowing pearl nestled in a crack in the ice above.

Layla gulped. The pearl was very high up, and the ice was very slippery.

Be *brave*, she told herself. *You're a Sea Keeper.*

They all started scrambling up the Frozen Falls, finding hand- and footholds in the ice.

"Keep going!" Marina urged them on from the water. "You're nearly there!"

But when they were halfway up the wall of ice, they heard Effluvia's voice singing her magic song:

"Listen to this siren daughter,
Melt those falls back into water!"

The Frozen Falls instantly began to melt, making the ice even more slippery.

"We're not going to make it in time!" Layla panted. The piece of ice she was clinging to broke off, and she had to grab another to stop herself from falling.

"Yes, we are!" Grace said determinedly, climbing even faster.

Layla looked up. The ice around the pearl was melting. Before Grace could reach it, the Golden Pearl slipped out of the frozen ice and fell...down...down...down...

"Catch it!" Layla cried in warning.

Holding on to the ice with one hand, Grace stretched out her other and—PLOP!—the pearl landed in her palm! "Got it!" she called out.

Emily and Layla scrambled farther

 8 9

up the melting ice until they could reach up and touch the pearl their friend was holding.

"I wish the sanctuary was fixed!" Layla said breathlessly.

The girls felt a magical mist spiral around them, and the golden light in the pearl faded away until it looked like an ordinary white pearl. A moment later, the frozen waterfall melted with a gush and the girls tumbled into the freezing water below.

"Marina!" Layla yelled as they fell. "HELP!"

Layla felt a shock as the icy water engulfed her. Her snowsuit was heavy and wet, dragging her down, and she couldn't breathe...

Suddenly she felt the fizz of mermaid

magic surrounding her, as her legs trans-
formed into a tail once again.

"WAHOOOO!" Grace cheered as
she surfaced, still holding the pearl. She
splashed the water with her tail and the
droplets froze in the air and fell around
them like diamonds.

"We did it! We found the Golden Pearl!"
Emily cried with happiness.

Grace handed the pearl to Marina.

"You can take this back to Atlantis to show the king and queen."

"I bet you think you're so clever," Effluvia sneered as she and the orca appeared at the surface.

Layla laughed. Actually, she did. She might struggle with schoolwork sometimes, but she was great at being a Sea Keeper. She grinned with pride.

"Just you wait," Effluvia spat out. "I'll get the next pearl, and then you'll be sorry!" She turned to Fang and the orca. "Let's go!"

The orca shook his head. "I'm not going anywhere with you!"

Looking more closely, Layla saw that the enchanted light had gone out of the orca's eyes. *The Golden Pearl's good magic has broken Effluvia's spell*, she thought happily.

The orca swam off with Effluvia chasing after him, shouting, "How dare you disobey me?"

As they vanished, Layla realized there was someone else missing. "Where's Harper?"

"There he is!" Marina pointed as Harper appeared at the surface.

"You were amazing!" Emily said.

"We couldn't have done it without you," agreed Grace.

"Did the magic work? Is the sanctuary fixed?" the narwhal asked.

"Let's go and find out!" Marina said. "And there's something else we have to do at the sanctuary."

"What?" Emily asked.

"Celebrate!" The princess's face broke into a smile. "Arctic merfolk love to party!"

Chapter Eight

The Ice Palace Animal Sanctuary, now back to its full glory, glittered in the water, its turrets gleaming like diamonds. Layla grinned as they swam into the great hall, which looked even more beautiful than before. The ceiling had been restored with intricate carvings of Arctic creatures. Luminous algae and shining starfish lit the enormous room with a warm glow. Huge ice sculptures decorated the floor, and mermaids crowded around a long buffet table overflowing with crystal clear bowls of ice cream.

"I can't believe I ever thought the Arctic mermaids were scary," Emily whispered as they swam over to the buffet table.

"Are these going to be seaweed-flavored?" Layla joked, wrinkling her nose.

Marina laughed. "This is *seafern* ice cream," she said, showing them a dark green one.

"I don't suppose you have any choco-late instead?" Grace asked.

"Just try it!" Marina said, laughing. The girls all took a tiny spoonful, expecting it to taste like spinach. But it was deliciously cool and minty.

"Frostberry is my favorite," Marina

told them, swimming over to a bowl of pale pink ice cream.

The girls swam from bowl to bowl, trying them all.

"Mmm, frostberry is my favorite too!" Layla exclaimed. It tasted like a cross between raspberry and pineapple—fruity and refreshing.

Suddenly, music started, and merfolk floated up in the water and began to dance. The girls grinned. Now they knew why the great hall was so tall—the space above the tables was the dance floor! As whale song filled the water, the mermaids danced together in complicated movements, swimming over and under and around in a brilliant display of flashing fins and tumbling tails.

"Come join us!" Toklo called.

But Layla had noticed something.

She nudged her friends. Anji was sitting down at one of the benches, looking serious as she talked to Harper. As soon as the Arctic mermaids had heard about the little narwhal's bravery, they had forgiven him.

The girls swam down to join them.

"Are you okay?" Emily asked.

"Sea Keepers! Thank you so much for saving the sanctuary," Anji said.

"And guess what!" Harper said, his fins fluttering with excitement. "Anji said I can stay here until I'm older!"

"That's great!" Layla grinned.

"I'm going to tell Marina!" Harper shot off to the dance floor.

Harper was delighted, but Anji looked worried. "Are you okay?" Emily asked.

Anji sighed. "The sanctuary is okay, but for how long? The Arctic is still in grave danger. The ice is still melting, and every little bit that disappears means less home for the creatures who live here." She sighed. "Can you ask the humans to help us?"

"We'll try, but we're only kids," Grace said sadly. "Grown-ups don't always listen to us."

"I'm young too, but I became the Arctic mermaids' leader," Anji said. "No one is too small to make a difference."

"I promise we'll do everything we can," Layla said.

"That's all we can ask," Anji told them.

As the Arctic mermaid hugged them, Marina came over.

"I must be getting back to Atlantis," she said. "And you should probably go home too." The girls nodded.

"Oh no!" Layla groaned.

"What?" Grace asked.

"We've still got to do our homework!" Layla moaned dramatically.

Emily and Grace giggled. It seemed funny to be thinking about homework after having an amazing mermaid adventure!

Marina hugged them goodbye. "I'll see you as soon as the Mystic Clam remembers where another Golden Pearl is," she promised. The girls hugged Harper and waved goodbye to the others. Then Marina sang a song, her voice surrounding them with mermaid magic:

"Send the Sea Keepers back to land,
Until we need them to lend a hand."

"Goodbye, Marina!" Layla called.

A moment later they were back in her bedroom, as if nothing had happened.

"Wow!" Grace said with a grin. "That was so cool!"

"We met some incredible creatures," Emily said. "I just wish we could do more to help them."

"Maybe we can," Layla said thoughtfully. "Come on, I've got an idea!" She ran downstairs.

No time had passed while they were mermaids, so Nadia and Dad were still cooking in the kitchen, and Mom was there too, getting a drink of water.

"You know how some kids are going on strike from school to protest about global warming?" Layla asked her parents.

Mom and Dad looked up and Nadia even took out her earphones.

"Well, I think we should organize a strike at our school," Layla said. "There are a lot of creatures around the world having their homes ruined by global warming. The polar bears and the narwhals can't change things, but we can. We need to show that it matters to us. That it's not okay."

Mom and Dad glanced at each other.

"Besides, it's our homework," Layla added. "We're supposed to do a project telling people about global warming, but instead of just talking about it we want to *do* something. That might actually help stop it!"

"We'll ask our parents too," Emily said.

"Yeah, I'm sure Mom will let me," Grace said, nodding.

"I've got Friday off. I can help organize it with the school..." Dad suggested.

"Okay!" Mom said finally. "But you need to catch up on all the schoolwork you'll miss."

"We will!" Layla said. "Thank you so much!" She hugged her parents.

"Well done!" Nadia looked impressed. "When did you get to be such an ecowarrior?"

Layla grinned at her fellow Sea Keepers. Then they hurried up to her bedroom to get started straight away.

"Anji would be proud!" Emily said.

"Well, there's a very good reason we have to keep the Arctic safe," Layla said, her eyes sparkling with mischief.

"For the mermaids and the animals?" Grace asked.

 105

"Yes, but also because I want to go back for more frostberry ice cream!" Layla joked.

The girls laughed as they began planning their school strike. They would do whatever they could to help—because that's what being a Sea Keeper was all about!

Dive in to more adventures with the Sea Keepers!

How to Be a
Real-Life Sea Keeper

Would you like to be a Sea Keeper just like Emily, Grace, and Layla? Here are a few ideas for how you can help protect our oceans and the environment.

1. **Reuse rather than recycle.**

   If you are done with a plastic container, clean it and find another way to use it instead of recycling it.

2. Plant a tree.

Trees produce food and oxygen. They help conserve energy, clean the air, and assist in fighting climate change.

3. Volunteer for a neighborhood cleanup.

Collecting litter and disposing of it properly keeps it from damaging soil or washing into lakes, rivers, and the ocean.

4. Hang clothes on a clothesline outside rather than using a dryer.

This saves electricity and energy.

Dive in to the next Sea Keepers adventure!

Chapter One

Grace took a deep breath and looked down at the bright blue water. She was standing with her toes at the edge of the swimming pool, the familiar smell of chlorine in her nose, and her swimming cap tight over her long, blond hair. At the side of the pool, her coach gave her a thumbs-up. Grace never normally felt nervous, but her team, the Dashing Dolphins, had been training for this competition for ages and she really wanted to do well. She shook her hands and legs, trying to loosen up.

"Go, Grace, go! Go, Grace, go!"

Grace grinned as she heard her best friends chanting. She looked up at the stands and finally spotted them. Layla was wearing a glittery top that caught the light as she jumped up and down, and Emily was twisting her curly hair around her finger. Next to them was Grace's mom, her hair in a messy bun and her glasses perched on the end of her nose, her granddad with his bushy white hair, and her little brother, Henry, who was in his swimming shorts and waving at her. "Just do your best!" Mom called, crossing her fingers. Grace nodded and pulled the goggles down over her eyes.

"Take your marks," the announcer

said. Grace raised her arms over her head and focused on the water. "Ready...go!"

As the horn sounded, Grace dove into the water and kicked as hard as she could. She knew she was a fast swimmer—but was she fast enough? She was aware of the girl in the next lane pulling ahead of her. If only she had a mermaid tail, she could have won the race without any effort at all!

Grace tried to concentrate. She couldn't be a mermaid, but maybe she could *think* like one. Shutting her eyes, she imagined that she had to swim as fast as she could, because there was a shark chasing her! Grace kicked her legs and pulled her arms through the water, imagining sharp teeth gnashing right behind her. She kicked her feet harder and harder, swimming faster and faster—until suddenly she touched the side of the pool. Catching her breath, she heard a cheer from the stands. She'd won!

"That was incredible!" her coach said, hurrying up to her with a towel as she pulled herself out of the pool. "That was your personal best!"

"And the winner is Grace Ryback!" the announcer cried.

In the stands, Grace's friends and family were all cheering. Grace rushed over to them, dripping and grinning.

"You swam like a mermaid!" Mom said, wrapping her in a big hug.

"There's no such thing as mermaids," Henry scoffed.

"I wouldn't be so sure!" Granddad

said, his eyes twinkling. "Did I ever tell you about the time my fishing boat was caught in a storm and I heard the most beautiful singing..."

Mom grinned and shook her head as Granddad started telling his tale, Henry staring up at him wide-eyed. As Granddad talked, Grace caught Layla and Emily's eyes and they shared a secret smile. They knew that mermaids were real...because they had met them!

It had started when they'd rescued a dolphin from a fishing net. But Kai was no ordinary dolphin, he was the pet of a mermaid princess. Princess Marina had taken them to Atlantis, an underwater kingdom, hidden from human eyes by mermaid magic. Atlantis was in grave trouble, because an evil siren called Effluvia was threatening to take over the kingdom. To everyone's surprise, the three human girls had been chosen to become Sea Keepers—the only ones who could find the magical Golden Pearls and use their power to stop Effluvia.

"Go and get changed, Grace," Mom interrupted her thoughts. "Henry's going to have his first lesson and then we'll all go home for dinner."

"I thought you could already swim, Henry?" Emily said.

Henry stood up and showed her his flippers, waddling along like a penguin. "I can! I'm learning to be a scuba diver!" he said excitedly, giving her a gap-toothed smile.

 117

"He's not old enough to actually scuba dive," Grace's mom told them, "but he's going to start snorkeling. He's got his assessment with the teacher today and then he starts lessons next week."

"It's going to be great. I'm going to see lots of fish. Hey—I bet you don't know why the jellyfish blushed." Henry put a snorkel on. "Mmm-mam bur bua GAH!"

"What?" Layla said, laughing.

"Why *did* the jellyfish blush?" Emily asked curiously. "There's a jellyfish called a pink meanie, but I don't think it's pink because it's blushing...?" She watched a lot of nature documentaries and knew lots of animal facts.

"Noooo!" Henry took the snorkel out of his mouth. "The jellyfish blushed because

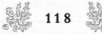

the sea WEED!" Laughing, he waddled over to where the sub-aqua club was setting up their scuba diving gear. Layla giggled.

"I can't believe I fell for that!" Emily groaned. Grace laughed as she took off her swimming cap and shook out her wet hair. As she did, she noticed something amazing—her shell bracelet was glowing!

Layla gasped and Emily turned to them both with wide eyes. Their bracelets were shimmering too. That meant it was time for another mermaid adventure!

"Um, I need to get dressed," Grace said hurriedly.

"I'll come with you!" Layla said.

"Me too!" Emily agreed.

"Great, see you back here. Henry won't be long," Mom said.

"Okay!" Grace called as she, Emily, and Layla hurried away.

"The Mystic Clam must have remembered where another Golden Pearl is hidden!" Emily whispered as they rushed into the changing rooms and ducked inside a cubicle. No time would pass in the human world while they were away, but they didn't want anyone to see them magically disappear.

Grace grabbed her friends' hands as they looked down at their shining shell bracelets.

Together, they chanted:

"Take me to the ocean blue,
Sea Keepers to the rescue!"

Bubbles appeared in the air, swirling and surrounding them with magic. The air sparkled blue as the bubbles spun faster and faster. Then—POP!—they were underwater, the scales on their tails glittering in the crystal-clear sea. They were mermaids again!

About the Author

Coral Ripley is the pen name of an author who works in children's publishing and has written a number of successful animal books. She cares passionately about the environment and the future of all creatures, big and small. Coral lives in London with her husband, baby daughter, and two cats.